Dear Parent:

Your child's love of reading starts here!

Every child learns to read in a different way and at his or her own speed. Some go back and forth between reading levels and read favorite books again and again. Others read through each level in order. You can help your young reader improve and become more confident by encouraging his or her own interests and abilities. From books your child reads with you to the first books he or she reads alone, there are I Can Read Books for every stage of reading:

SHARED READING
Basic language, word repetition, and whimsical illustrations, ideal for sharing with your emergent reader

BEGINNING READING
Short sentences, familiar words, and simple concepts for children eager to read on their own

READING WITH HELP
Engaging stories, longer sentences, and language play for developing readers

READING ALONE
Complex plots, challenging vocabulary, and high-interest topics for the independent reader

I Can Read Books have introduced children to the joy of reading since 1957. Featuring award-winning authors and illustrators and a fabulous cast of beloved characters, I Can Read Books set the standard for beginning readers.

A lifetime of discovery begins with the magical words **"I Can Read!"**

Visit www.icanread.com for information on enriching your child's reading experience.

Be safe! Always cook with an adult. Don't touch
sharp knives or hot stoves and ovens! And always
wash your hands before and after cooking.

And this one is for you, Felix!
—S.G.

I Can Read® and I Can Read Book® are trademarks of HarperCollins Publishers.
Balzer + Bray is an imprint of HarperCollins Publishers.

Otter: Best Cake Ever
Copyright © 2021 by Sam Garton
All rights reserved. Printed in the United States of America.
No part of this book may be used or reproduced in any manner whatsoever without written permission except
in the case of brief quotations embodied in critical articles and reviews. For information address HarperCollins
Children's Books, a division of HarperCollins Publishers, 195 Broadway, New York, NY 10007.
www.icanread.com

ISBN 978-0-06-299120-1 (pbk. bdg) — ISBN 978-0-06-299121-8 (trade bdg.)

21 22 23 24 25 LSCC 10 9 8 7 6 5 4 3 2 1
❖
First Edition

My First — SHARED READING

I Can Read!

OTTER

Best Cake Ever

By SAM GARTON

BALZER + BRAY
An Imprint of HarperCollins*Publishers*

Today is Teddy's birthday.

We are baking a cake.

Shh! Don't tell Teddy.

What kind of cake would
Teddy like?

Giraffe wants to make
a tall cake.

Pig wants to make a
pink cake.

Robot wants to make a
square cake.

I have a better idea.

Shh! Don't tell Teddy.

First we all wash our hands.

Then Otter Keeper gets
a big bowl.

Giraffe puts in butter.

Pig puts in flour.

Robot puts in two eggs.

I put in some sugar.

I mix it up. I am good
at mixing.

We pour the mix into a tin.

It goes into the oven.

The cake smells yummy.

Now we frost the cake.

The cake is almost done.
The last step is top secret.

Shh! Don't tell Teddy.

Surprise!

Teddy loves his cake.

It looks just like him!

It tastes yummy.

I want to eat it all.

"No more cake today. Time to clean up," says Otter Keeper.

"I will stay with the cake,"
I say.

I think Giraffe wants
more cake.

Oh dear. I hope Giraffe
does not eat more cake.

Oh no! Somebody ate
all the cake!

Shh! Don't tell Otter Keeper.